CW00558525

E.E. Adams

Government and Rebellion

E.E. Adams

Government and Rebellion

1st Edition | ISBN: 978-3-73406-683-2

Place of Publication: Frankfurt am Main, Germany

Year of Publication: 2019

Outlook Verlag GmbH, Germany.

Reproduction of the original.

GOVERNMENT AND REBELLION.

A SERMON DELIVERED IN THE
NORTH BROAD STREET PRESBYTERIAN CHURCH,
SUNDAY MORNING, APRIL 28 1861,

BY

REV. E. E. ADAMS.

PUBLISHED BY REQUEST.

1861.

GOVERNMENT AND REBELLION.

An evil man seeketh only rebellion; therefore a cruel messenger shall be sent against him.—Prov. xvii. 11.

We have in these words this plain announcement—that Rebellion is a crime, and shall be visited with terrible judgment. Solomon here speaks his own convictions; God declares his thought, and utters his sanction of law. This is also the expression of natural conscience,—vindicating in our breast the Divine procedure, when the majesty of insulted government is asserted, and penalty applied.

God never overlooks rebellion against his throne—never pardons the rebel until he repent and submit. God does not command us to forgive our offending fellow-men, unless they repent. "If thy brother trespass against thee seven times in a day, and seven times in a day turn to thee, saying, I repent, thou shalt forgive him." God is in a forgiving attitude; so ought we to be. But he does not *express* forgiveness until the rebel expresses penitence; neither are we under obligation to *pronounce* an enemy forgiven until he signify his compunction and sorrow, and desist from his injurious conduct. If my child rebel against my law and my rightful discipline, I am not allowed by the spirit of love to pursue him with vengeance; neither am I bound by the law of God to release him from the penalty of his sin, until he shall have exhibited signs of submission, of sorrow, and of obedience. I may pity him, and cherish toward him the *spirit* of forgiveness; but for his own sake, for the order of the household, and on account of my innate sense of justice, I must not pronounce his acquittal, nor declare the controversy ended, until he shall have satisfied my governmental authority, and the sentiment of justice which both his own conscience and mine, constitutionally, and therefore by necessity, cherish. And I do not see that Government can safely pardon a rebel against its statutes, its honor and its common brotherhood, until his rebellion cease; until he

2

bow to law, confess his crime, and signify his sorrow. I speak not of oppressive government, of iniquitous law; but of *good* government, of statutes healthful, humane, equal. Although in the former case rebellion cannot be justified until every constitutional measure has been resorted to for redress,—then, if redress be not given, the voice of the people in all representative governments may legally change oppressive for just laws, and oppressors for rulers who shall regard the popular will. And in despotisms, when the people have the *power* to redress their wrongs, and to enter on a career of development in mind and morals, in the arts of civilization,—when every other course fails —"resistance to tyrants is obedience to God!" Man was not *made* for tyranny. He was not made for any form of government that crushes out his intellect and his religious capabilities. He was made to be governed morally; to be under righteous law; law which, while it restrains passion, selfishness and crime, gives a man all the freedom that he is able and willing to *use* safely for himself, and for the commonwealth; all that is consistent with individual development and the national good.

I am not one of those who believe that the voice of the people is, without exception, the voice of God. It was not so at the Deluge, but quite the reverse. It was not so when Israel clamored for a king—not in mercy but in anger, God gave them their request. It was not so when Absalom stole the hearts of the people, and stirred up rebellion against his father. And yet, when a nation, independent of party, free from the excitements of momentary interest, without the influence of ambitious leaders, under the calm guidance of reason, history, and the spirit of the age,—rises spontaneously against oppression, against iniquity, and *demands* just laws; rights for all; free thought, free speech, free labor, free worship; when compacts are not violated; when moderation is maintained; when the spirit of humanity is preserved,—then, I believe, "the voice of the people *is* the voice of God." I have no question that, in the great principle, Cromwell and his puritan hosts were right in their revolutionary action. I could never doubt that our fathers did a noble, glorious, and Christian deed in throwing off the yoke of Britain, and proclaiming a new government for themselves and their posterity. It was right to contend and bleed for equal representation, for freedom of conscience, and for an independent nationality in which these high ends could be secured.

The first government of which we have account was a Theocracy— that is, "the government of God." *He* was the only King. He revealed the law, appointed leaders, gave rules for worship, instruction and warfare. Thus in the outset did he set up his claims among men. He established the great precedent, which men ought to have followed, which the world has ignored; but to which the thoughts and the will of the race shall ultimately return. It is true *now* that government, as such, is ordained of God. All government, in its elemental authority, is a theocracy. All power is of God; he ordains law. He originates the idea of civil compact. While, therefore, the principles of governments among men may be defective, and the administration wrong and hurtful, the great *fact* of government is a *Divine fact. Good* government is *emphatically God's* government—intended to suppress evil, to promote holiness and happiness. "The powers that be are ordained of God." "Whosoever therefore resisteth the power, resisteth the ordinance of God: and they that resist shall receive to themselves damnation." Despisers of government are enumerated by the Apostle as among the most flagitious of men. There are *statutes* in almost every government which may not be absolutely right; some which may be oppressive. These are to be distinguished from the principles, from the general bearing of a government, and endured for the good therein, or be rid of by constitutional and safe methods. It is a duty of each subject and citizen to surrender some of his desires and preferences—some of his convictions possibly—for the *general* sentiment—the comprehensive good; while he has the privilege of convincing by fair argument all others, and winning them to his views and measures if possible, without violence, without infringement of law. It is not to be expected that every man should be absolutely satisfied with any government. If he is called to yield only his share of personal interest and preference, for the sake of all the protection and blessing in which he participates in common with the state, his reason, his conscience, his patriotism will joyfully acquiesce; he will freely make so much sacrifice for the interests of the whole, knowing very well that every other citizen is likely to be under an equal sacrifice. Natural, individual liberty, without law, is only barbarism. Where every man is free to do whatever his worst passions prompt, there is in fact no freedom; there is tyranny; for the strong will subdue the weak, bone and muscle will govern mind and conscience. In laws and governments men have their best thoughts; human *law* is likely to be better than human nature. Men feel the need of restraint—are convinced of the necessity of law. They therefore make laws in self-defence; if thereby they would *not* restrain their own selfishness, they *would* restrain the selfishness of others; but that which is made a barrier to *one* bad subject is also a defence against all;—thus men do restrain themselves by their defences against others. Thus it is that,

4

with healthful convictions, men may control diseased passion; with a right *ideal* is intimately joined a safe actuality; with good law, a comparatively good condition. Even in the worst administration, and when the public mind is most demoralized, there may remain the purity of law; the sublime thought. If the mind finds itself sinking into lawlessness and disorganism, and borne away by the pressure of evil, it can look upward, and, catching new energy from the unquenched light—

"Spring into the realm of the ideal."

Our destiny is ideal. We are on our way to the Unseen. The ideal draws us upward,—*real* now, to the spirits of just men made perfect—to be real to us when we are perfect—*once* ideal to them, as now to us. We must keep above us the model of life and of law which we have not yet attained. Let it never be dim. It is a star shining through time's night! A banner waving from the throne of God. It tells us of the goal. It points out our futurity—the altitude of our virtue, our exaltation, our bliss.

Our subject is GOVERNMENT AND MAN. We proceed to consider it in a three-fold aspect, inquiring

1. *What is good government?*
2. *What constitutes rebellion against such government?*
3. *What is the duty of each citizen when rebellion exists?*

I. WHAT IS A GOOD GOVERNMENT?

No citizen looks for an absolutely perfect form of nationality—of law. But we have a right to ask for good government. We have been accustomed to think that it depends more on administration than on principle; and the line of the poet, "That which is best administered, is best," is a proverb, to the sentiment of which we too freely yield. No doubt a government with bad statutes and wrong laws, may be so administered as to produce a tolerable degree of national comfort and development for a season; while a Constitution perfect in its theories and principles, may be so maladministered as to corrupt and distract, impoverish and demoralize, a people. And yet, I agree with an old patriot of the past century who said, "There is no foundation to imagine that the goodness or badness of any government depends solely upon its administration. It must be allowed that the ultimate design of government is to restrain the corruptions of human nature; and, since human nature is the same at all times and in all places, the same form of government which is best for one nation is best for all nations, if they would *only agree to adopt* it."

There is a deep thought in this remark. We often say, for example, "France is not fit for a republican form of government," and it is true; but that is *not* to say, "A republican form of government is not fit for France," if the population would agree to adopt and preserve it. Man, in his fallen state, is not fit for the holy government of God; but that holy government is, nevertheless, the *only* one that is fit for man as a moral being; and it is man's ignorance and folly, his guilt and ruin, that he does not adopt it. It is owing to the ignorance and wickedness of the world that it is not fit for a representative government; and that all do not choose Christ to be their King. Were a score of the professional politicians of our land to frame a Constitution for us in full accordance with their own schemes and choice, we would soon find ourselves under an oligarchy of schemers, who cared for the Republic only so far as to secure from it their own fame and emolument. Were as many brokers or merchants to make and administer our laws, without regard to other industrial interests, we should have an oligarchy of trade. Were as many husbandmen, or mechanics, or lawyers, to have full control of our legislation and government, we would have one interest towering above all others, and true equalization, true brotherhood, just representation, healthful nationality would be impossible. Or, were we dependent on officers in the army or navy for our government, legislative and administrative, we would be likely to have many of our rights circumscribed. Were as many clergymen to frame a Constitution, and administer laws, we might be under a crushing priesthood. A government of mere scholars, poets or orators, would be only a sublime dream. A Constitution of philosophies alone, would glitter with abstractions beautiful, cold, grand as the snow-capt Alps, and as distant, too, from the actualities of men! A government of mere gentlemen who have nothing to do but think for slaves, to enjoy the chase and the race-ground, to extol their pedigree, and traduce labor, and lead retainers to war—would be a government for the few over the many, an aristocracy of blood and privilege, of curled moustache and taper fingers; but not a republic of patriots, of self-made men, of equal privilege and just laws. It would be a return to semi-barbarism, to the age of Louis XIV., or even of Charles I.

This is now the strong tendency in the Rebel States: even along our free border, but below it, such is the system of representation, that a county containing only about 3,000 inhabitants, sends as many representatives to the legislature as another county of 30,000, and a single proprietor casts as many votes as a whole commune. So much liberty of citizens is already sacrificed to the chevalier, to the system of forced service.

But were a select number of experienced men, of true statesmen, embracing different pursuits and professions, educated in different parts of the world, and drawn together by grand national events,—statesmen born in the age when liberty had its first grand revival, and was guarded by soberness of thought, and tried by every variety and extent of sacrifice—by men who had no professional, exclusive interest to provide for, but who expected to fight and die for their convictions, who sought only to lay the foundation of a nationality for future generations, and for the world; who aimed at a healthful union of all popular interests, both among poor and rich, among masters and dependents; who provided for freedom of action under law; of worship and education, of commerce, agriculture, and the arts; for the easy and equitable support of government,—for its perpetuity indeed, infusing into it elements that appeal powerfully, both to the self-interest and the patriotism of the citizens,—I say, were such men, with such ends in view, by such sacrifice, to frame such a government, containing the most delicate balance of interests, with strong checks against the encroachment of any branch, either the legislative, executive or judicial, giving all trades and professions, and all men, an equal chance for excellence, influence, and honor; you would not hesitate to pronounce that a good government, even though you might find slight exception to some of its terms, though you might not interpret as others do, all its constitutional phrases.

In view of the protection which such a constitution affords, especially if it had been tested, for a period of eighty years, by all the inward strain of domestic evils, and all the outward pressure of invasion; by the influence of foreign envy, of intrigue, of hostility; by the debasing power of disloyalty, the incompetency of rulers, and the general degeneracy of human nature; I say, in view of all these untoward influences, the government which could still retain its majesty and power, still stretch its Aegis over every national and individual right—you would pronounce the best, both for ruler and people, that ever blessed a nation. And you would not hesitate to declare *that* man a *traitor*, who should attempt *to weaken* and destroy it!

Now we pretend to say that *our* government was thus formed by the choicest wisdom and patriotism of the world, with the largest liberty in view, under the restraint of law, giving equitable privilege to all its citizens, and so balancing its different departments that they are mutually a defence. We pretend to claim for our government the loftiest purpose, the most comprehensive views, and the best practical results. We claim for it justice, equality, and power. It does not stand out—a thing distinct from the people and the states. It is not an objective power only, but subjective; it is in every State and in every freeman. It is not in machinery, which can be set in motion and work out certain results, as if every part of it were iron or steel, and put into action by applied heat; but in *men*, in minds, in hearts, in the family circle, in the church, in every throb of patriotism, in every fibre of the husbandman and the artizan, in the pastor's prayers, and the student's living thoughts. It is in the *nation* like latent fire, like a hidden life— evoked in time of peril, and flashing along the telegraph, breathed in song, uttered in oratory, thundered from the cannon's mouth, hung out in streaming banners whose "every hue was born in heaven," felt in firm resolve, illustrated in response to the call of country and of law. Where is our government? Not at Washington alone. That is but its symbol. It is throughout all our Loyal States. It is enthroned on the granite hills of New Hampshire, sends its voice along the Alleghanies, and on the swelling floods of the Mississippi, and spreads its wing over the children of the West, even to the shores of Oregon. It lives in every cottage, and every mansion, and has a throne in every true, free, noble, Christian heart.

That it is a *good* government, you have only in imagination to blot from the face of the earth whatever has grown up under its protection and encouragement, by the will and the blessing of the Almighty, during the fourscore years of its existence; level all the cities, sink the commerce, prostrate the schools and churches, obliterate all the science, history and thought it has fostered, quench the light of oratory, turn back the wheel of improvement, and leave us at the opening of 1776; estimate all the freedom of act, of utterance, of industry; reckon the sum of human comforts, even of luxuries, it has brought to our hand. Look at all our ships, our mechanism, our homes, our sanctuaries, our institutions of morality, of mercy and of religion; our wealth, intelligence, order, power; consider the elevation given to millions in the worst form of civilization in the land, showing that such is the vitalizing force of our national life, that even slavery here, bad as it is—and we know of nothing worse as a system—lifts men above the natural license of savage existence. Consider all this, and much more, that I may not stop to utter, and you cannot—you *do* not—no sane mind *can* question the supreme excellence—I had almost said the *divine* excellence—of our government. And if there were need of other proof, we have only to remind you with what promptness the call of our noble Chief Magistrate was answered from every free State—from the city and the hamlet; from the bank, the bar, the press and the pulpit; from the workshop and the soil; from the calm and comfort of home and ease and affluence, and from the cottage of the poor, as if the pulse of the government were beating in every vein, and the will of the Cabinet had its home in every bosom! Strong men, young men, aged men, men of leisure, Christian men—all ready to march under the stars and stripes, or to pour out their treasure for others. Mothers and wives and sisters, with breaking hearts and tremulous benedictions, bidding the heroes go—offering them on their country's altar. Oh, it would not be thus but for the true manhood which our government infuses into loyal citizens. It would not be so, but for the Christianity it protects without dictation, and acknowledges without ostentation.

II. WE COME NOW TO THE QUESTION, *WHAT CONSTITUTES REBELLION AGAINST GOOD GOVERNMENT?*

There may be criminal rebellion even against a wicked and oppressive government. The people may take the law into their own hands, and put to death, or imprison their rulers, without *first* having tried constitutional methods of redress. But I speak of rebellion against *good* government—such as we have already had in review. There is a difference between insurrection and rebellion. The former is an act of a people or population against a single statute, or against a portion of the legislative enactments, without necessarily growing into warfare, or revolt against the whole constitution and the laws. This may become rebellion. There is also a difference between rebellion and revolution. The latter, in a political sense, is a change, either wholly or in part, of the constitution. This may be effected by argument and a peaceful vote—by abdication, by a change of national policy in view of some new relation, and by general consent, or by warfare. "The revolution in England in 1688, was occasioned by the abdication of James II., the establishment of the House of Orange on the throne, and the restoring of the constitution to its primitive state."

Our revolution of '76, and onward, was not a rebellion; it was resistance of oppression, of burdensome taxation without equal representation, and it resulted in our distinct nationality.

The revolutions of France have been of a similar character; they have sprung from oppression of the most severe and unnatural kind. This was the fact, at least, in 1797 and in 1830. In 1848, when it was my lot to be in the midst of it, the revolution arose from the selfish conduct of Louis Philippe, who enriched himself and his family out of the national treasury, and encouraged his sons in a course which was at war with national precedent, with the commercial interests and democratic individualism of the French; for with their imperial prestiges and tastes they are extreme in their personal democracy.

But all these revolutions resulted in good to the people. Education, public spirit, enterprise, labor, all the arts of civilization, and even evangelical Christianity received a new impulse. Mind was opened and enlarged; the people thought for themselves, and sighed for knowledge and a better faith.

Revolution is going on silently, from year to year, in England. The nobility yield by slow, almost imperceptible degrees, to the demands of the people. It is by this process that the Government avoids the shocks which startle Austria, France and Italy.

Such is the variety of honest opinion among men on all subjects; so different are the degrees of information, and the opportunities of judging with regard to the best measures of government; such a diversity exists in the interests and abilities of a people,—that they may be good citizens without being satisfied altogether with the constitution, or with those who administer its laws. There will be different political parties. It is the glory of a government that the people are allowed to think and vote as they please, and to express their honest opinions. Perhaps with us, expression is too free, especially in regard to public men and measures. We may have diverse views and convictions, and yet feel and act loyally. But men who endeavor by any influence or means to lessen the loyalty of others, to alienate the love of the people from the government, and who signify their own aversion, not by condemning a single statute and seeking its lawful repeal, but by heaping abuse on the constitution and on those who are chosen to administer the laws, by avowing their hostility to the government and its policy, or their purpose to resist and war against it, —are in a posture of rebellion. Those who, being in office, commanding the arms and other property of the government, cause them to be removed so as to weaken its power and strengthen those in actual rebellion, or who are threatening the same; those who aid and comfort a population or soldiery who are in a state of actual resistance, and finally, those who do openly and avowedly renounce the authority of the government to which they have sworn allegiance, or take up arms to attack its strongholds, seize or destroy its property, or injure the soldiers and citizens who are sent to protect it,—are in a state of rebellion against its laws and against the commonwealth over which it holds the shield of its authority.

Korah was a rebel and a traitor, who having, by intrigue, inspired some other leaders with the spirit of sedition, succeeded in drawing from their allegiance to Moses and Aaron, a large number of the people, who came together in a mob to demand a different administration. They were invited to refer the matter to the Divine decision, but they stoutly refused, accusing Moses of assumption, thus endeavoring to destroy his authority over the nation. That was rebellion. Again, in the reign of David, his son Absalom drew the people from their allegiance, then seized the reins of government and pursued his father with an army. That was rebellion against wholesome law, against the will of

God.

Now we have the painful fact before us, that rebellion has sprung up against our good government. Men in many quarters have secretly plotted, and openly avowed hostility to our Federal Union. Eight of our States have passed the Ordinance of Secession, four or five others are assuming an attitude of hostility to the General Government, or refusing to comply with the Executive, who calls on them to aid in the defence of the Capital. This state of things has been preceded by acts of treachery on the part of leading men in the States, by seizure of arms, money, and public defences,—the property of the government. A new Confederacy is formed, contrary to oaths and compacts, for the purpose of destroying our Union, and giving perpetuity to slavery. It has attacked our forts, adulterated our coin, stolen our arms, proclaimed piracy against our commerce, set a price on the head of our Chief Magistrate, threatened our Capital, and raised armies to exterminate, if possible, our nationality. And all this it has done without one act of the Government to provoke such procedure; without any oppression; without any threat; but in the face of every honorable proposal on our part, after long and patient endurance of their encroachment and plunders; even until foreign journals deride us for our forbearance, and the rebels themselves insult our delay.

There are those who have compared this rebellion with our revolution of '76. There could hardly be a wider distinction, both in principle and in fact, than between these two movements. The Colonies, had been oppressed by "navigation laws," intended by the British Parliament to crush out their commerce for a whole century, from 1660 to 1775. Their weakness during that period did not allow of resistance. They were taxed oppressively, while they were not allowed a representation. This was in violation of Magna Charta; for the government of Great Britain was representative. Having been aided by the Colonists during the Seven Years' War, in the subjugation of Canada, the Parent Government—without asking taxation through the regular action of the Colonial Government—assumed the right to tax our expanding commerce, and commenced a vigorous enforcement of revenue laws. "Writs of Assistance" were issued, whereby officers of the king were allowed to break open any citizen's store or dwelling, to search for, and seize foreign merchandise; sheriffs also were compelled to assist in the work. The sanctions of private life might, by this act be invaded at any time by hirelings; and bad as it was in itself, it was liable to more monstrous abuse. Then came the "*sugar bill*," imposing enormous duties on various articles of merchandise from the West Indies, and greatly crippling Colonial commerce: then the infamous Stamp Act, by which every legal instrument, in order to validity, must have the seal of the British Government—deeds, diplomas, &c., costing from thirty-six cents to ten dollars apiece: then the duty on tea; and, finally, the quartering of soldiers on our citizens in time of peace, for the express purpose of subjugating our industry and energy to the selfish purposes of the crown.

It is enough to say, that the rebels against our Government have suffered no oppression. They do not set forth any legal ground of Secession. The government has done nothing to call out their indignation, or to inflict on them a wrong. They have had more than their share of public office; they have had a larger representation, in proportion to their free citizens, than we have; they have been protected in their claims, even against the convictions of the North; we yielding, as a political demand, what we do not wholly admit as a Christian duty. We have assisted them by enactments, by money, and by arms, in the preservation of a system at war with our conscience, and with our liberties. We have paid for lands which they occupy; and after all their indignities and taunts, and attacks on our citizens, their plunders, and their warlike demonstrations, we have been patient; and are even now imposing on ourselves restraint from the execution of that chastisement, which many of their sober and awed citizens acknowledge to be just, and which, if the call were made by the Executive, would at once be hurled on the rebels by an indignant people, like the rush of destiny.

Now, I grant, for I do not wish to make the matter worse than it is against them, that in the North, individuals have demanded more than the South were able, at once, to give. Some have pushed reform faster than it would bear, faster than the laws of Providence would allow; but it was honestly and conscientiously done. We have sometimes in our warmth, uttered irritating words; but all this has been returned by blows, and by savage vindictiveness. We have shown a willingness, of late, to yield some things; to abide by the sense of the whole people; but these States are, by their rulers, declared *out of the Union*, without appeal to the people; they have commenced the war, and now they are regarded by the whole world as in a state of rebellion, not of justifiable revolution. They would submit to no method of adjustment that we could honorably allow. They desired war, as they have been for years preparing for it, at the expense of the Government, and in its service and trust, drawing their life from the bosom which they now sting; and because freedom will no longer bow, as it has done for a whole generation, to their will, they rebel, proclaim a system of piracy, and threaten the subjugation of the whole American people. It is a deep, and long determined treason, running into the whole national life, and is become to ourselves a question of *personal* liberty.

III. WHAT THEN, WE ASK, *IS THE DUTY OF ALL CITIZENS WHEN GOOD GOVERNMENT IS ASSAILED BY REBELLION?*

Doubtless, *one* duty is to inquire whether they have in any way contributed criminally to the occasion or the causes of such rebellion; whether they have demanded too much of the disaffected, or encouraged a wrong spirit in them by coinciding with views leading to their present attitude; whether they have participated in any way with a policy calculated to irritate, to defy, to provoke honest minds to anger? Whether as individuals, as Christians, they have been bitter and harsh, and vengeful, or are so now; and if they find any such spirit, it becomes them to repent, and school themselves into Christian charity and moderation. But, notwithstanding any possible error in the past, the Christian citizen must consecrate himself to the defence of the government and its *policy*; for however, there is a distinction ordinarily between the two; in a crisis that involves a nation's life, the policy which would save it, is the spirit of government and order.

The true Christian will pray, and speak, and write, and labor, and die for its success! Will give assurance of his sympathy and support, and refuse to do any act that can be construed into *comfort* to the rebels. He will encourage troops called to support the government, and its policy, giving them food, clothing, advice, BIBLES AND ARMS. He will rouse their patriotism, and call down on them the benediction of heaven. This is the duty of ministers, and magistrates, of churches and individual Christians. And if the rebellion continue, it is their duty to advocate and help to form armies of sufficient numbers and power to utterly subjugate the rebels, and, if they cannot otherwise be brought to submit, put an end to their existence. That is what God did by the hand of Israel, to Korah and Absalom; and it is the legitimate issue, if needs be, of all successful resistance,—of all defensive warfare. To deny it, is to deny the right of self-defence. It is to put a man in a position where he must love his enemy better than himself and children, which even Christianity does not demand, though it does enjoin forbearance, charity, and sacrifice. To deny this is to condemn the principles of our Revolution, and to sanction the plunder and destruction of national property and being.

What, therefore, is our duty, now that rebellion actually rages against our mild, equal, good Government—the best, on the whole, that the world ever saw? rebellion without cause; with no legitimate ground of offence; rebellion for the sake of a dark and demoralizing system, that has robbed half the nation of its conscience, and cursed it with an inveterate idolatry. What is our duty? What is mine as a citizen, a Christian, a minister of God—as a man? What is yours? Plainly to ask, What have I—either by demanding too much, not in abstract right, but in the light of present possibility—contributed towards this fearful condition? What by my love of money, my sanction of oppression, my apologies for wrong, my complaint against government, my support of wrong principles, my neglect to vote and pray for the right, my boast of national greatness, my worship of power and neglect of goodness, my forgetfulness of God? What by all these, and more that I do not think of, have I done palpably, possibly, toward bringing on this terrible crime against justice, humanity and law? Then it is my duty to repent of all this and deplore it. It is also my duty to strive against personal hatred and revenge, and to pray for my country's enemies just as I would for my own, and *because* they are my own—not that they prosper in their rebellion, but that they repent and find mercy, and acknowledge the authority against which they are at war. It is our duty specially to pity and pray for the multitudes of good citizens and their families, who cannot escape from among the rebels, and who are in great jeopardy; men who love law and the Constitution, and the whole country; who are either resisting, under the greatest pressure, the evil that is upon them, or yielding through fear and force. We feel for them; we call them our brothers. But it is also my duty and yours to support our government—our administration; to pray for and sympathize with our President and his Cabinet in their most trying posture, in the midst of such perils, and with so meagre means for the moment, of establishing order, and setting the nationality in permanent security. It is our duty to report traitors to the police, that they may be lawfully cared for; to help our militia and volunteers with every comfort and defence; to hold up the arm of government so long as rebels remain.

This is *our* country, bought with blood. It is second only to the redemption which Christ purchased for us! And if we are called to contend with principalities and powers, and spiritual wickedness in high places, for the safety of our souls, surely we may contend with flesh and blood, with rebels and traitors, to save this glorious inheritance from the gulf of anarchy and the bonds of a lasting servitude. *War is terrible*, but slavery and plunder and the silent gangrene of national dishonor, bribery and perverted conscience are worse. The burst of a thunder cloud may break down a forest of lofty pines, but the slow delving of the mole may undermine a thousand habitations. The secret corrosions of the ship-worm will sink a fleet.

This deep-working, inward ruin is appearing on the face of society. The stupendous fact is, that from Baltimore, onward throughout the disaffected States, the population is under the guidance of mad leaders, and exposed to mob power. Thousands of good citizens are flying to us for protection; thousands more forced into the war against the country, and other thousands sighing and praying in secret that God will give success to our arms and rescue themselves and their families from ruin. For these, as well as for our liberties and honors are we summoned to war; it were a crime to be inactive. The Bible is militant. Christianity is a warfare with sin. Life is militant,—a perpetual fight with death. If our blessings are worth praying for and praising for, they are worth *fighting* for, and if not to be otherwise secured, *must be fought for*.

I want this country to live! I want my children to grow up under its shield! I want to see constitutional liberty mount above the obstacles of ages, and rise higher and higher here, I want Italy to look toward us now with hope! I cannot bear to hear the cry of shame that will come over the Atlantic from the vineyards of France, from the glaciers of Switzerland, and from the steppes of Russia, if we permit the walls of our blood-bought inheritance to be broken down. For the sake of God, liberty, religion, all over the earth, I want our flag to be honored abroad.

In the French revolution of '48, a deputation came to me to demand the American church at Havre, for the purpose of holding a political meeting, I refused. They intimated that it would be torn down. I had only to assure them that I would plant our flag on it, and if they touched it with rude hands, they would have to answer to our government. That was the last of the matter. This power we must have still; and to secure this the whole North and West must awake, and act—for the multitudes who in the Border States demand our aid; for the thousands of laboring, suffering poor who tremble beneath the glance of the proud chevalier; for the sake of our education, our lands, our homes, our Christianity. We are sure that success on our part now will demonstrate to the world the inherent power of our nation. They cannot behold the united action and offering of *nineteen millions* in the free States—all animated with the spirit of liberty, religion and law, and resolved to crush treason and rebellion at any cost—without a deeper conviction of our real might, without a new impression of the majesty that reposes in a people's will! All Europe approves of this war; and struggling nationalities look with anxious expectancy for the issue.

It is a war for government, for order. It is against the power and rage of the mob, led on by ambitious men who are mad at the loss of power. There is nothing more sublime than law; holding unseen the hearts and interests of millions, protecting their rights, and giving them full, happy development. Our flag represents law, liberty, sublime sacrifice, national life. It is therefore right even for the Christian to fight for its perpetuity. If I may defend myself and family, the nation is greater than my family and myself; and calls more powerfully for my service. And this war, entered on by necessity, and with the grand purpose of protecting order and law, and rescuing a whole population from ruin, is inspiring in its motive, and therefore elevating in its influence. We are consciously better, nobler, in proportion as we forget ourselves in the sublime idea of our nationality, and all that this nationality can do. When men fight for plunder, or victory alone, they labor downward, they become brutish; but a war for true liberty, for national life, for our homes and our inheritance, and for the oppressed, is elevating, purifying. War is terrible in itself, and in some of its consequences, but there is a bow on the cloud. When the bolt has spent itself in the pestiferous air, all nature is bright and glorious. With true discipline, soldiers are made vigorous in body; they are also quickened in mind by the tactics and incitements of warfare, they are ennobled by high motives, and may leave the campaign better than when they entered it. Courage is awakened; love of liberty and order inspired; benevolence increased; and loyalty exalted by this war. What men bleed for they value. I have been delighted with the eagerness with which many soldiers whom I have visited, listened to Christian address, and received the word of God. It is a matter of gratulation that but few arrests are made in our city in these days, not because the police are less watchful, but because the debased portion of the population are inspired with a better thought. It is also hopeful to find, that many who entered our city as volunteers, or as drafted soldiers, are actually being reformed from their evil habits, under the greater strictness of camp discipline.

We are cheered also by the fact that the people generally are more earnest than formerly in their attendance on divine worship; more solemn, and full of feeling, and disposed to study the Bible, They need God. They look to God. We all feel the Bible to be more than ever precious. Its solemn prophecies are swelling into fulfillment. The day of

God is approaching, and the kingdoms of the earth are giving way for the coming of the Great King!

The feeling is, and ought to be, intense for the conflict. Let the question be decided. Let half a million of freemen be called, when the time shall indicate, to form a line of fire along the boundary that separates Secession from loyalty. Let them take up their mighty march through the revolted territory, if it will not otherwise submit, and proclaim as they go, "Liberty throughout the land!" Let the flag that waved over the suffering heroes of Valley Forge, and the conquerors of Yorktown, wave forever on the Capitol, and over every village and subject in the land! Nay, it must be so. We must bow, if we do not conquer. They have proclaimed it. Come down, then, from the Northern mountains, and out from the forests and the fields, ye sons of the Pilgrims, with your firm force of will, and your achieving arms! Come up from the marts of commerce, ye daring children of the Empire State, and ye firm hearts of New Jersey and of Delaware! Come forth from the echoes of Erie, and the shores of Michigan and Superior! Come from the free air of Western Virginia and Ohio, from the loyal districts of Maryland, Kentucky, and Tennessee! Come forth from the great West! and with them, go, ye strong and true of my adopted State and City, who listened even in your cradles, to the bell which gives out its tones over the birth-place of our liberties! Go forth, and live the epic that future ages shall sing: be yours the glory of *rooting this treason out*! And as they go, bless them, aged fathers with tremulous voice! and mothers, bid them God speed! wives and sisters and Christian hearts, load them with your gifts and your prayers! And when they are gone, remember them at the home altar, and bless God that your country does not want defenders; and when your tears are dried up, and your cause is proclaimed triumphant, weep again tears of joy as you clasp the returning heroes to your arms! Or, if they shall be borne home to you wounded and worn in their country's service, be grateful that your eye can watch over them, and your hand minister to their necessities and griefs. Or finally, should they fall in battle, you will have the consolation of knowing that they saved your country; that they did something to consolidate its strength, and illustrate its glory before the world. For we are destined to conquer,—and after this trial the nation will come forth as gold. We need to suffer that we may value our liberties. From the valley of tears arise notes of victory and hallelujahs. Nations as well as saints, come up out of great tribulation.

"None die in vain

Upon their country's war-fields! Every drop
Of blood, thus poured for faith and freedom, hath
A tone, which from the night of ages, from the gulf
Of death, shall burst, and make its high appeal
Sound unto earth and heaven."

The motto now is—"No compromise! *Submission!* Give up the leaders of rebellion! Bow to law! Nay, more—no longer *ask* us to protect your dark system!"

But it is possible that, while we stir ourselves up to a fierce belligerency against rebellion, and rush into hot condemnation of those whom we once called *"brethren," we* are rebels against God! Some of you who are equipping for the war, and ready to take the field in defence of your country and her laws, are in heart at war with holiness and God! You may see in the fever of our whole population what men think of treason against a good earthly government! See also in the commands of God, in the life and death of Jesus, in the declared interest and anxious watchfulness of angels, in the whole glorified army that shall attend the Great King when he comes to set up his final assize,—what the Principalities and Powers in Heaven think of your treason against the holy government of Jehovah! Behold in the uplifted arm of Justice—hear in the voice of the Judge, what shall be done to him who will not repent! Now the offers of pardon are made through the death and sacrifice of Jesus. Repent; forsake your sin; lay down your arms; retire from your rebellious attitude; and from the throne of Mercy shall the fact be proclaimed, that *you* are pardoned and restored!

Lightning Source UK Ltd.
Milton Keynes UK
UKHW010041070223
416578UK00002B/142